I0741958

COUNTING

ONE TO TEN

Written by Stacey Abrahams — Illustrations by Alyanna Janica Lumagui

FOR ADULTS WITH ALZHEIMERS
dementia & memory loss

A note from the author

I would love to take the opportunity to thank friends and family who have supported me throughout this journey. To acknowledge my friendly and caring co-workers who remain strong and positive while working to ensure each of these adults feel safe and at home in their environments.

I invite you all to visit our Facebook page;

https://www.facebook.com/MattersOfTheMindBooks/

..and follow for updates about further releases of books and products.

To open and like our Facebook page please scan the below QR image with your phones camera to open it up into your browser.

If you have any feedback please leave a review on the Facebook page. It would be lovely to hear stories about any reactions or memories raised from reading with the book that you feel comfortable to share.

OPENING
DISCUSSIONS

Read the book, identifying the images
as you go counting from 1 to 10.

Display the images one at a time and where appropriate ask:

- **What is this 'image'?**

- **Where would you find this 'image'?**

- **How this 'image' is used?**

- **Have you used this 'image' before?**

Share one of your own memories or a story about one of the images as an example.

Then invite others to join in if they have a memory about one of the images that they would like to share.

ONE

PRAM

2

TWO

ELECTRIC

TOASTERS

THREE

VACUUMS

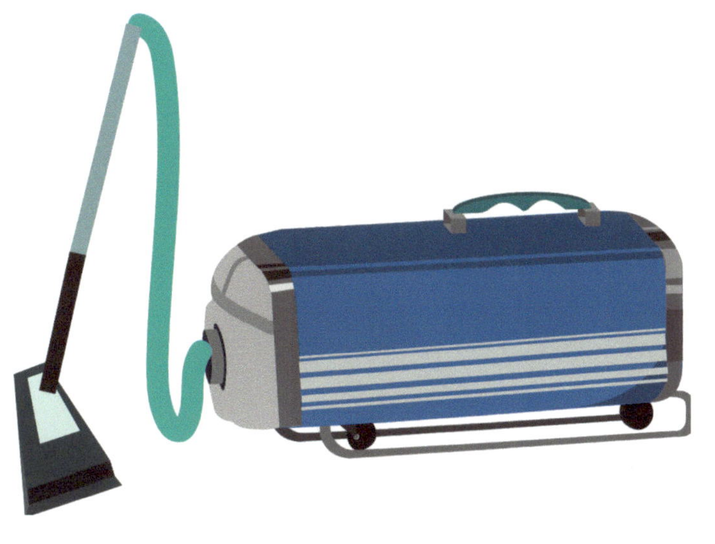

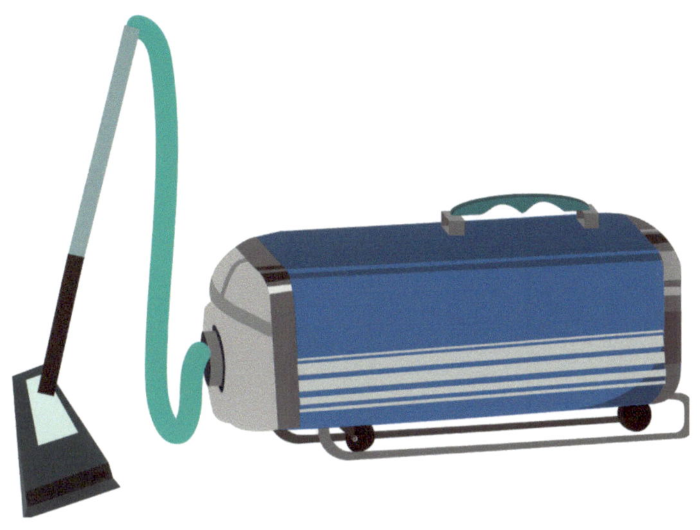

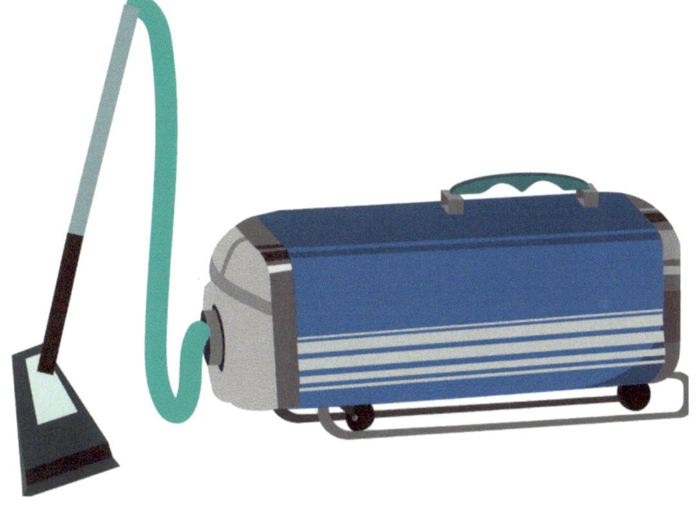

FOUR

WASHING

MACHINES

FIVE

RECORD

PLAYERS

SIX

IRONS

7
SEVEN
TRAINS

EIGHT

BUSES

NINE

PLANES

TEN

CARS